The King who came back

The King
who came back

by Avraham ben Yaakov

FELDHEIM PUBLISHERS
Jerusalem / New York

Illustrations by Avraham Kaufman

First published 1984
ISBN 0-87306-355-4

Copyright © 1984 by
Avraham Greenbaum

Phototypeset at the Feldheim Press

Philipp Feldheim Inc.
200 Airport Executive Park
Spring Valley, NY 10977

96 East Broadway
New York, NY 10002

Feldheim Publishers Ltd
POB 6525/Jerusalem, Israel

Printed in Israel

For
Rachel Rivka
and
Yeshayahu Gedalyahu Yakir

אֲזַמְּרָה לֵאלֹקַי בְּעוֹדִי

תהלים קמ״ו ב׳

There was once a kingdom where the people were always happy. The king was very wise, and he gave good laws to his people. It was a land of truth and justice, where everyone loved his friend as much as himself. The people did their work happily and spent their days singing songs of praise and thankfulness to the king.

One day, the king decided to teach his people a great lesson. He summoned them all to the gates of the Royal Palace and announced that he was leaving the country to go on a long journey. He promised faithfully that he would surely return. And he told the people that while he was away they should follow his wise laws and lead their lives in goodness and purity. He told them that he was leaving behind two Counselors to guide them in his absence. If any problems were to arise, the two Counselors would offer their advice. And the people should choose and do what was right and just.

The first Counselor was wise and goodly. His face shone with a gentle, kindly smile, and his words were soft and sweet. The second Counselor was young and handsome. He was everybody's friend. He would come up and put his arm around people's shoulders and talk about every subject under the sun. And he liked it when people liked *him* and liked how handsome and friendly he was. But truth to tell, he was somewhat foolish.

The king reminded his people to follow his laws and be happy. Then all would be well. The people cheered, and the king bade them farewell. And then he was gone.

The people of this country loved the king so much that each morning and evening they gathered together to sing his praises. Every morning, before they did anything else, groups of people would come together in meeting halls all over the land to greet the light of day with songs sweeter than those of the birds, sweeter than the music of the flowers and trees, sweeter even than the song of the stars. And as darkness fell they would gather again and sing praises so radiant that even if a person were burdened with troubles, his soul would rise up and shine in the blackness of night. The people would leave these meetings refreshed and strong in their love for the king, and determined to lead their lives in devotion to his laws.

Now the king had gone, but as the days went by, the people faithfully gathered in their meeting halls morning and evening. They sang their songs of praise and joy, as was their custom. Yet something was not quite the same. Their joy was somehow not as perfect as it had always been before. The people *tried* to sing with the same happiness and devotion. They reminded themselves that the king would soon be back and that the best thing would be to follow his laws and live in purity and goodness. But the king seemed so far away. The people didn't feel as close to him as before. And in their hearts they were uneasy.

The days passed. The people continued to gather each morning and evening, but something was lacking. The Elders of the people became worried, and they decided to request a meeting with the two Counselors whom the king had left behind. So a meeting was arranged between the Elders and the Wise and Foolish Counselors.

The king had a certain Enemy who had long ago been banished from the kingdom. All through the years he had tried every kind of plan to return. But as long as the king was in his land there was never any place for the king's Enemy. Because the one thing the king's Enemy couldn't tolerate was happiness, and in this land the people were always happy. So all his plans had come to naught, and he was forced to wander from country to country, wherever the people were anxious and unhappy.

But all through the years, the king's Enemy had very cunningly sent a sack of gold each month to the king's Foolish Counselor. The sack of gold would arrive mysteriously at the Foolish Counselor's house, and with it there was always a little note written in spidery handwriting: "Tell no one where this came from."

Once in his life the king's Foolish Counselor had seen the king's Enemy. It was a sight he could not forget. His face was green and creased with terrible wrinkles and furrows. His cheeks were hollow. His eyes were like black pits. Just a glance at his face was enough to make one's heart sink with fear and depression.

Each month when the sack of gold appeared, the king's Foolish Counselor would remember that face, and he trembled. He dared not tell a soul where the money had come from. But it was gold after all—and the thought of all the things he could buy would cheer him up. He would make a big party for all his friends, and they would eat and drink and sing late into the night.

The day arrived for the meeting of the Elders and the king's two Counselors. In the great square in the center of the capital, facing the Royal Palace, stood the Grand Council Chamber. Inside the Chamber at the front were the two Counselors. The Wise Counselor sat calmly with a gentle smile on his face. The Foolish Counselor happily welcomed all the Elders, slapping them heartily on the back, shaking them by the hand and asking how they were. The Wise Counselor rose and addressed the meeting.

"It is good that you have come, my dear friends, to discuss the affairs of our country. For now that the king has left us for a time, we must strengthen ourselves and remember his wise advice. If we are happy and follow his laws, leading our lives in goodness and purity, everything will surely be well with us."

So sweet were the words of the king's Wise Counselor that the Elders soon felt there was nothing to be worried about at all. They had only to look at the kindly smile on his face and listen to his soft, reassuring voice and they felt a glow of warmth and joy in their hearts.

But while the Wise Counselor was speaking, the Foolish Counselor suddenly noticed something moving in the shadows at the back of the Chamber. He peered forward to see what it was. And peering back at him out of the gloom was the green, furrowed face of the king's Enemy! The Foolish Counselor nearly fainted. He was terrified of the face and terrified that someone might discover he had received all that gold from the king's Enemy. He tried not to show how frightened he was.

Suddenly the ridiculous thought entered his mind that the king would never come back. He knew it wasn't true; it was absurd. But he couldn't help letting a deep, worried frown pass across his face. Then something dreadful happened. Try as he might to smile as though nothing had happened, the lines of that frown were marked on his face as if someone had gone over them with a black pen. They stayed there and they wouldn't go away!

The Elders were of course seated facing the king's Counselors, so they couldn't see what was happening at the back of the Chamber. All they could see were the king's two Counselors. When they saw the look of anguish on the face of the Foolish Counselor, all their own fears returned. After the Wise Counselor finished his speech, one of the Elders rose to his feet and said, "It is true, honored Counselors, that the king gave us good advice while he was still here. But now that he has left us, the people feel so *far* from him. They simply don't feel as happy as they used to. . . ."

While this Elder was speaking, the Foolish Counselor suddenly noticed that a crumpled-up piece of paper had dropped into his lap. He unfolded it, and a golden coin fell out. A look of terror passed across his face, and he quickly hid the coin in his pocket. But the lines and furrows of that look of terror had also become inscribed on his face. No matter how hard he tried to smile so as to show that everything was all right, the lines remained. The message on the paper was in the same spidery handwriting he knew so well.

"Tell no one where this came from. You will be richly rewarded. The king is not going to come back. Why not ENJOY YOURSELF!"

The Foolish Counselor looked to the rear of the Chamber and again he saw the green face peering back at him out of the gloom. He tried to smile—but it wasn't his natural hearty smile. He pulled his cheeks into a grin and crinkled up his eyes, but his face was as taut as stretched elastic. And worst of all, the lines and wrinkles of that false smile were also penciled into his face.

He said to himself, "I can't believe that the king isn't going to come back, because it's the king's Enemy who's saying he won't. It's no good my being so frightened. It'll soon make me old and ugly. The king wanted us to be happy, and I *should* enjoy myself. We *all* should!"

When the Elder who had been speaking sat down and the king's Wise Counselor was just about to answer him, the Foolish Counselor broke into a broad smile, beamed at everyone and cried out cheerfully, "What's everyone worried about? Brother Elders, we can't spend our lives being worried. After all, the king wanted us to be happy! I've got a plan."

The Elders looked towards the Wise Counselor, who sat patiently with a grave expression on his face. The Foolish Counselor continued, "The king wanted us to be happy. I propose that we should give everyone a special holiday. They can spend the day thinking about the king and remembering how good things were when he was here. Everybody will enjoy themselves and then everything will be all right!"

A buzz of excitement went around the Chamber and some of the Elders started clapping. The Foolish Counselor was delighted that they agreed with him and he forgot about his worries. Then the Wise Counselor rose to his feet.

"My dear ones, it is true that the king advised us to be joyous always. Only think carefully. If everyone has a special holiday, it will be pleasant, perhaps, while it lasts. But afterwards it will soon be forgotten and no one will be any happier. *My* suggestion is that in order to remember the true greatness of the king we should take more time over our daily meetings. We should think carefully about what the words of the songs we sing mean. Then we will remember the joy we used to feel. And I propose that twice a week, every Monday and Thursday morning, we should sing special songs about how much we long and yearn for the king to come back — and he *will* return before long."

The words of the Wise Counselor seemed very sensible. Just as he was finishing his speech, however, a hissing sound was heard in the Council Chamber.

The Foolish Counselor went white with fear. When the Elders saw him they were afraid. But the Foolish Counselor soon recovered himself and said, "Don't be frightened. My friend's words are very wise, as usual. Far be it from me to disagree with him. But I still think we all need a holiday to begin with. It'll cheer us all up — and then we'd be more in a mood to follow his suggestion. Well, my fellow Elders, what do *you* think?"

The Elders agreed, and it was decided that a national holiday should be declared, and that on Mondays and Thursdays extra songs would be added at the morning meetings to mourn the king's absence and long for his return.

The day of the national holiday arrived and the people enjoyed it immensely. They ate and they drank, and things seemed almost as good as in the days when the king was there. There was nothing much to *do*, so the day did seem a little long. People ate and drank even more, and some of them got indigestion.

The next day things seemed as drab as they had been before, especially to those who had eaten too much. The day after that was a Thursday, and everyone spent extra time at the morning meetings, just as the Wise Counselor had proposed.

As they sang their songs about the greatness of the king they remembered his radiance and glory, and a feeling of longing pulled at their hearts. They thought how far they were from the king, and they were filled with sorrow. Tears came to their eyes and they yearned for the day he would return. But the extra songs did seem a little long for a few of the people. They couldn't concentrate all the time and their minds began to wander. They couldn't help thinking about when the next national holiday would be held and how they would enjoy themselves again!

The days passed and the meetings continued as usual, morning and evening. But certain people began wondering whether there was all that much point in singing the songs very carefully since the king was so far away. Could he hear them, after all? They never thought of *not* singing the songs—they'd been singing them all their lives! But they started paying less

attention to what the words meant.

Before long it was as if they were just going through the words to get the songs finished and over with. And that just made the meeting seem even duller. One or two people started coming late in the mornings, or even staying in bed so late that they would miss a meeting altogether. And quite a few became so bored during the singing that they started chatting about clothes or business or other things which had nothing to do with the meetings.

The Elders were worried where all this might lead, so they requested another meeting with the king's two Counselors. Once again they gathered in the Grand Council Chamber, and the Wise Counselor rose to his feet.

"My dear ones, you are right to be concerned about the feelings of the people. For the king taught us that nothing is more important than joy. Only when people are unhappy and anxious can the king's enemies gain strength. Now more than ever we should think deeply about the greatness of the king. We will surely be filled with happiness and joy when we realize how fortunate we are to have the honor of being his subjects."

The words of the Wise Counselor were true, and the Elders felt a bit happier when they heard them. But all of a sudden, in the middle of his speech, a very rude noise was heard. It seemed to have come from the back of the Chamber. The Elders of the people were shocked at such a disrespectful interruption to the words of the Wise Counselor. But the Foolish Counselor really did find the noise very funny, and he couldn't help smiling. He quickly forced his face into a serious expression. But the lines of that cheeky smile had already been written on his skin.

The Wise Counselor continued:

"We should all spend more time thinking about the wisdom of the king and the just laws he has given us. When we realize the truth of his guidance and teachings, we will also realize that he was surely telling the truth when he promised faithfully to return. And he *will* return before long."

Suddenly, there was another rude noise. And this time the Foolish Counselor found it so funny that he couldn't help laughing out loud. But when he saw how shocked the Elders were, he quickly pretended he was smiling because he'd had a bright idea.

"I know what!" he shouted. "I've got a great idea. It's true what the Wise Counselor says. The people do need to realize just how great the king was. But it's hard for them with the king so far away. The people need something *real* to help them remember how great and kind he was. Here's my idea: the king was so wealthy—his estates stretch for miles and miles. His treasure houses are stuffed with all kinds of wealth. He left all his possessions in my charge. In order that everyone can see for themselves how wonderful he was, I propose we open up his fruit orchards and every household in the kingdom will receive a basket of fruit as a gift from the king's treasury!"

There was a flurry of excitement in the Council Chamber. The Elders were overjoyed that the king's Counselor cared so much about the needs of the people. Of course, they were anxious to see if the Wise Counselor would agree to the plan, but just as he was about to stand up, there was another rude noise.

The Foolish Counselor burst out laughing again. To hide the fact that he was laughing at the noise, he pretended he was happy to have suggested such a marvelous plan, and he forced his face into a broad smile. Indeed, it was such a broad smile that his cheeks ached. When he released them, they had stretched so much that they sagged and drooped.

Before the Wise Counselor could say a word, the Foolish Counselor cried out: "Let's have a vote!" The Elders enthusiastically voted in favor of the proposal, and no one even noticed that the king's Wise Counselor had left the Council Chamber.

The Foolish Counselor was delighted with himself for proposing such a clever plan, and before long he was telling everybody what to do to prepare for the distribution of the fruit.

The Elders were still not sure if it was right to go ahead with such a plan without asking the advice of the king's Wise Counselor. When they realized he had gone, a messenger was sent out to look for him. But the Wise Counselor was nowhere to be found.

"We can't just wait here doing nothing," said the Foolish Counselor crossly. "This is an emergency. Who knows what might happen if the people don't get the fruit. Quickly! You've got to help me!"

The Foolish Counselor glared at the Elders with a very fierce and important look on his face. But this just added new lines and furrows to all the other wrinkles and creases that would remain inscribed on his face in the years to come.

But there was plenty to do without thinking about the future. The Foolish Counselor had to attend to everything himself now that the Wise Counselor had disappeared. Announcements had to be posted explaining to all the people in the kingdom when and where they should assemble to receive the fruit. Thousands of baskets had to be prepared. The fruit itself had to be gathered from the king's orchards, which meant hiring extra workers to pick it, sort it and put it into the baskets.

For days the Foolish Counselor scarcely had time to eat or sleep. There was only one thing he could always find a few moments for. Ever since he had first realized how handsome he was, he loved to look at himself in the mirror. Each morning, after washing his face, he would gaze at himself and see once again how *nice* he looked. This would fill him with fresh happiness and enthusiasm. Off he would go like a friendly puppy, certain that everybody else would find him equally nice and likable.

Only these days, as he looked in the mirror, he couldn't help noticing that his once-handsome face was getting rather obviously marked with an unpleasant array of lines and wrinkles. The very first time he had seen them he thought they must be creases brought on by the way he had slept the night before. He tried patting the wrinkles and smoothing them out, but they wouldn't go away. He pulled his face into a friendly smile till the muscles ached, but the lines and wrinkles were still there. As he stared and stared at them his heart sank. With a feeling of horror he remembered that green, hollow face peering back at him out of the gloom. It was a thought he couldn't bear. So he pulled his face into the broadest smile he could manage and went rushing off angrily to carry on with the arrangements for the fruit distribution.

First thing next morning, he went back to the mirror, hoping his fresh, handsome face would be back to greet him this time. But it wasn't. The lines were still there—and added to them were the lines from all the cross, angry, bossy looks he had worn the previous day. Again he tried smoothing them and rubbing them, but they still looked back at him accusingly. He stamped his foot in anger and spent the day rushing even faster to try and stop any worrying thoughts from entering his mind.

The Foolish Counselor tried to console himself with the thought that when the big day came for the fruit distribution, *he* would be the one to hand it all out. How the people would love him for giving them all that fruit! He sent a message to the Elders telling them it was important that the people should realize that the fruit was a gift of the king. Since *he* was the king's Counselor, *he* should be the one to give it out. They should all come to the gates of the Royal Palace, where he personally would hand them their fruit.

When the day came, the Foolish Counselor enjoyed himself tremendously, slapping the adults heartily on the back, kissing the children and beaming at everyone as he gave out basket after basket to the lines of people. "Don't worry!" he cried, "the good old king won't let us down! There's plenty more fruit to keep us going till he comes back!"

The people were delighted. The basketfuls of grapes, dates and figs, apples, oranges and pears made a wonderful change from their everyday food, which seemed very ordinary by comparison. They were overwhelmed by the generosity of the king and his Counselor. For the next few days they really did sing their songs of praise at the daily meetings with feelings of thankfulness and joy . . . until all the fruit was eaten up. Then their everyday food seemed duller than ever. The songs of praise became flat and hollow again. So the Elders requested another meeting with the king's Foolish Counselor.

This time he sat alone at the front of the Grand Council Chamber. Elder after Elder made speeches urging him to distribute more fruit. But the Foolish Counselor was hardly listening to a word of what they were saying. All he could see was that lurid green face with its sunken eyes staring back at him out of the gloom.

He leapt to his feet and shouted angrily, "What am I supposed to do? I can't go on giving out all the king's fruit! There won't be enough!"

One of the Elders said that they wouldn't need to use up all that much fruit because the king would be coming back soon, wouldn't he?

But the Foolish Counselor shouted back, "Who said? Suppose he doesn't come back soon! Suppose he *never* comes back!"

The Elders were stunned into silence. It was the first time any of them had even *thought* that the king might not return. Even the Foolish Counselor himself was shocked that he had said it openly.

He tried to cover himself and continued hurriedly, "Well, I was only trying to be practical. I mean we can't go on giving out all the king's fruit for nothing. I want you to have fruit as much as anyone!"

Suddenly the Foolish Counselor beamed with pride.

"I know what! We *will* give out more fruit. But in order to pay for it, the people will have to work. That's fair, isn't it? We'll give out another basket of fruit to every family in the land. But in order to cover the cost, all the adults will have to spend one afternoon working in the king's orchards."

The Elders were still feeling quite shocked, but they couldn't deny the facts. One Elder was worried, however, and he asked if the king would mind all the people coming into his orchards without his permission.

Just as he asked his question, a rude noise was heard from the back of the Chamber, and the Foolish Counselor laughed loudly. It was a harsh laugh which left sharp lines on his jaws and around his eyes.

"And who asked for your opinion?" he shouted fiercely. "In any case," he cried, "you can go and tell the people they're *helping* the king by tending his orchards."

None of the other Elders was in the mood to raise more questions about the plan. So all the adults duly spent an afternoon working in the king's orchards, and at the end of the afternoon each one received a ticket allowing him to come to the next fruit distribution outside the Royal Palace.

Once again the Foolish Counselor handed everyone a basket of fruit, and again he enjoyed himself thoroughly. So did the people. True, the baskets of fruit were rather smaller than the time before. But it was fruit, after all. And when everything else in life was somewhat drab and dull, the fruit made a pleasant change. It wasn't long before the people were pressing the Elders for another fruit distribution and the Elders were asking for a meeting with the Foolish Counselor.

By the time this meeting took place, the Foolish Counselor had been doing some arithmetic. It was quite obvious to everyone that fruit would have to be given out on a regular basis. Even if all the adults were to work one afternoon a week in the orchards, that still wouldn't be enough to ensure sufficient fruit supplies. When the Foolish Counselor suggested they should all work *three* afternoons a week, the Elders thought it would be very burdensome.

"Well, it's up to them," said the Foolish Counselor coldly. "If they want fruit they'll have to work for it. Otherwise they won't get any."

The Elders shrugged and obediently raised their hands in favor of working three afternoons a week.

It wasn't more than a few months before the number of afternoons had to be increased to four each week. Then it was five. And before long all the adults were having to spend six afternoons every week working in the king's orchards. This was in addition to their usual work.

Life became a rush. Every morning at daybreak, the people would hurry out to their morning meetings. No sooner had they assembled than they would all start reeling off the songs one after the other. No one had so much as a moment to collect his thoughts. Gone were the beautiful melodies of the past. In their place was a single, monotonous, mournful dirge.

On Mondays and Thursdays there were the extra songs of longing and yearning to be got through. But no one had the time to shed a tear, even if he thought about what he was saying. As soon as the last song was finished, everyone would rush home to grab a bite to eat before running off to their usual jobs and getting through their work as quickly as possible. They had to hurry to get to the orchards in time, because anyone who was late got a black mark on his ticket for the fruit distribution, and that meant that he received less fruit.

By the end of the day, their heads were spinning. When they arrived breathless at the evening meetings it was as much as they could do just to get through the words of the songs and praises. To say them nicely or to think of their meaning would have been too much. Even before they finished the last words they would start getting ready to race back home, grab a bite to eat and fall into their beds exhausted.

The fruit distribution days made a welcome change from the routine. But even they were painful occasions for anyone who had any feelings left. The pressures of their lives had made everyone selfish. All they could think about was the fruit they were going to get. They would push forward to collect their baskets and everyone would check how much he had got and look jealously into other people's baskets to see if they had been given an extra pear or a banana, an orange or a fig.

"I was here before you!" people would cry, or "You deserve less than I do. Last Wednesday, at the orange grove, you were late!" Everyone was angry with everyone else, and people hardly looked at each other's faces any more. They hardly spoke to one another either, because they didn't have the strength. And in any case, what was there to say, except that the figs were wormy or the apples bruised, the grapes were half-rotten and the bananas brown?

As for the Foolish Counselor, he was in a worse state than ever! Each morning when he looked in the mirror, the grooves and furrows and wrinkles and creases had become even uglier. His cheeks were becoming sunken from exhaustion and over-work. His eyes were hollow from sleeplessness. Smile and preen as he might, nothing made him look any better. His heart would sink and he would rush away from the mirror and throw himself even more furiously into his official activities.

He had a thousand and one things to think about, and he

could scarcely pay attention to anyone. But one day, as he was rushing around the orchards on a tour of inspection, he happened to hear someone groan, "How long can this go on?"

The Foolish Counselor was furious and screamed, "How dare you complain! You've never had it so good! You certainly never had fruit like this in the old days." He bellowed at the supervisor to find the man's ticket, and furiously scribbled black mark after black mark on it.

But late that night the same question kept asking itself again and again in his mind as he tossed and turned on his bed trying to fall asleep. "How long can this go on? How long can this go on?" And all he could see, as his sleepless eyes darted from shadow to shadow in the darkened room, was the image of that green, lurid face which brought such terror to his heart. He screamed at his attendant to come and light up the lamps. When the attendant was gone again, the Foolish Counselor sat before the mirror contemplating his own haggard face.

"Suppose the king *does* come back!" he thought to himself. "Then I'll certainly be disgraced and banished! And what if he doesn't? What future will there be for me?" And his throat choked with tears at the thought of how ugly he was becoming. He pulled his face and tried to stretch the skin to see if he could make himself look handsome again. But nothing worked. "Why?" he asked. "Why am I so unhappy?"

All at once, he knew the answer.

"It's because I'm not *enjoying* myself enough!" he cried. And suddenly he gasped, and his careworn eyes lit up for a moment in triumph.

"I've got it!" he cried, "I've got it!" And with an evil whisper he said to himself, "I know what I'll do. Yes. I know what I'll do!" At that moment he decided:

"The king is *not* going to come back."

The next morning, the Foolish Counselor summoned all the

Elders to the Grand Council Chamber. When they were all assembled, he gestured for silence and rose dramatically to his feet.

"Elders of the people," he announced gravely, "I have some very serious news to tell you. Last night I received a message from the king himself. He informed me that he regrets he will not be returning to our country. He advises you to choose me as your king instead, and wishes you all the very best."

The Elders were silent.

"Well? Do you agree?" asked the Foolish Counselor, as if he needed reassurance. No one said a word.

"Good!" he screamed. "Now get back to your work."

The Elders were ushered out of the Council Chamber by a number of not very pleasant looking attendants, and the Foolish Counselor hurried back to his house to make arrangements. Within hours he had moved into the Royal Palace. It was only a matter of days before notices were plastered all over the capital announcing that the new king's coronation would be held on such and such a day. And to celebrate it, everyone would receive an extra bunch of grapes!

The Foolish Counselor had gone out of his mind, and no one in the kingdom had either the time or the courage to puzzle out what was happening.

In the countryside, far away from the capital where all these events had been taking place, there lived a farmer simple and honest. In all his ways he followed the laws of the king. Six days he worked and on the seventh he rested. When the harvest time came he separated his tithes and gave gifts to the poor, and then he sat down to eat the fruits of his labors in gratitude and joy.

Years went by. The farmer's wife gave birth to a baby boy,

and the farmer brought him up to follow the ways of simplicity and truth. He couldn't teach him arts and sciences—he didn't know them himself. "But there's one thing," he said to his son, "that is more important than anything else: always tell the truth."

In the summer the farmer would take his son around with him and show him the wonders of nature. And when winter came and the nights were long, they would sit together by the fireplace, and the farmer would tell his son about the greatness of the king. He would describe the splendor of the capital, with its wide avenues and fine squares. He would recount the magnificence of the king's court, with the throngs of courtiers in their gorgeous costumes. He would tell him of the clothes of the king himself: how glorious were the colors of his robes—the blues, reds, purples, gold and silver; and how exquisite were the different fabrics—the silks, brocades and satins. And then he would describe the countenance of the king: the radiance of his eyes and the splendor which shone from his face.

What the farmer had words for he would describe in glowing detail. And when the words failed him—for after all, he was only a simple man—he would gesture with his hands as if to say how the greatness of the king was just . . . indescribable. And his son, David, would dream and wonder. How he longed to go up to the capital and witness that glory! How he yearned to catch sight of the garments of the king and glimpse the radiance of his countenance.

The years passed and David grew older. Here on the farm they heard little of the events which had altered the face of the capital. They knew that the king had gone away for a while, and once messengers had come from the king's treasury demanding extra taxes to pay for the fruit distributions. The farmer had cheerfully agreed, because he was sure that if officials of the king were making such a request, the extra taxes must be necessary and good. And in any case, with thanks to God he had plenty to spare. He was only too honored to be able to make a contribution to the king's treasury. All he had to do was to abide by the king's laws and tell the truth and then all would be well.

David was almost thirteen years old. Long before, the farmer had decided that on David's thirteenth birthday he would take him all the way to the capital in order to witness its splendor and glory. It was true that the king was not there for the moment, but from the magnificence of the capital and the royal palace David would at least get a faint idea of the true majesty of the king himself.

The farmer prepared a horse and loaded a cart with provisions for the long journey. Several days before David's birthday the farmer and his son set off in the direction of the capital.

After a three day journey they could at last see the ramparts and towers of the royal city gleaming in the distance. David was so excited he wanted to carry on without stopping until they arrived. But his father said they should spend the night on the outskirts of the city. The following day was David's birthday, and they would celebrate next morning by entering the city with their minds fresh and ready to enjoy the splendor of the royal capital.

Early next morning they awoke and said their prayers. After eating some of the food they had brought, they left the horse and cart in a safe place and set off on foot for the final stage of their journey. As they drew nearer to the city they could hear the sounds of crowds of people. The farmer told his son how happy the inhabitants of the capital were to live so close to the splendor of the royal court.

When they entered the city they found that the streets were filled with people all hurrying in the same direction to the center of the city. David asked his father why they all looked so tired and anxious. The farmer said they must have been busy performing the will of the king. They all had bags in their hands, and they were pushing and jostling one another and pressing forward as fast as they could.

The farmer caught sight of a huge notice headed by the royal crest:

> AT 11 O'CLOCK TODAY THE KING WILL RIDE IN PROCESSION THROUGH THE STREETS OF THE CAPITAL AND GENEROUSLY GIVE FRUIT TO HIS LOYAL SUBJECTS.

The farmer was overjoyed! The king must have returned suddenly and the news of his arrival hadn't reached them there on the farm so far from the capital. Things couldn't have worked out better. David would be able to have a glimpse of the king himself. It was a gift beyond their wildest dreams! And the farmer said that if the king was going to give fruit to the people, it was a sign of his wonderful generosity. He and David had no need of the fruit, of course, as they had brought plenty of provisions for themselves in the cart. They made their way forward with the throngs of people in order to get a view of the royal procession.

The grand square was an enormous area flanked by the gates of the Royal Palace, the Grand Council Chamber and the other ceremonial buildings of the kingdom. Leading from the gates of the palace was a wide avenue which had been roped off for the procession. Along the sides of the avenue were numerous platforms piled high with all kinds of fruits. And on every platform there were guards armed with staves, keeping the crowds back. Some of the people cried out, "Fruit! Give us fruit!" But the guards barked out: "Not till the procession! Only if you cry out 'Long live the beautiful king!'"

The farmer and his son made their way to the front of the crowd. Suddenly a fanfare of trumpets was heard and the gates of the Royal Palace swung open. A roar went up from the crowd. "Fruit! Fruit! Give us fruit! We want fruit!"

"See how the people are cheering!" said the farmer to his son, and they leaned forward excitedly to catch the first glimpse of the royal procession.

First came guards on horseback: the guards wore gold and scarlet uniforms, and the horses were crested and plumed. Then came a series of silver and golden carriages loaded with grapes and figs, dates and pomegranates, apples, oranges and pears. Standing on each carriage were eight uniformed soldiers, and as a fanfare of trumpets sounded, they cried out, "Long live the beautiful king!" and tossed a few pieces of fruit into the air. Someone in the crowd shouted back: "Long live the king!" and the soldiers immediately threw fruit in his direction. Some other people began shouting the same words, and they also had fruit thrown to them. Soon everyone was shouting out: "Long live the beautiful king!" and fruit rained down on the entire crowd.

At last the king's carriage itself appeared. It was an open carriage made entirely of gold and studded with rubies and sapphires and emeralds. Upon it stood a figure swathed in robes of majesty and splendor. The crowd shouted, "Long live the beautiful king!" as they pushed and scrambled to pick up as much fruit as they could.

But when David caught sight of the face of the figure in the king's carriage, he could hardly believe his eyes. Its cheeks were hollow, its eyes were sunken and lifeless, and its greenish-yellow skin was marked with the most hideous furrows and wrinkles and creases.

"But he's ugly," David cried. "How can this be the king? He's not beautiful at all! He's ugly!"

"Shhhhhhhhh!" said the people in the crowd next to him,

turning to him with shocked and frightened faces. "Long live the beautiful king!" they shouted.

"But it's not true!" cried David. "He's ugly!"

The people looked at him angrily and signaled him to keep quiet.

"No!" he cried, "this isn't the king. It can't be!" And he tried to see what his father was saying, but his eyes were blurred with tears. He couldn't see his father, and the surging crowd was sweeping him along. "Long live the beautiful king!"

"No!" cried David. "This isn't the king! He's ugly! He's ugly!"

The people began poking and shoving him, but he couldn't stop himself. All his life he had learned to tell the truth. Blows were raining down upon him, but he kept on crying, "It isn't the king! It can't be! It can't be!" He pushed and struggled to get out of the crowd. At last he broke away and started running. He had to get away. He ran and ran until he came to the outskirts of the city. He kept running through the meadows and fields until he came to the hills. Still he continued running until he came to the uplands and saw the mountains in the distance. At last, exhausted, he threw himself down on the ground and fell into a deep sleep.

When he awoke, the sun was shining and the birds were singing. It was peaceful and tranquil there in the hills. He heard the ripple of a flowing stream and went to drink some water. He gathered some berries to eat. Then he sat on a rock and began to think about the strange events he had witnessed.

After a time he became aware of the sound of a voice singing. The song was sweet and pure. David climbed down from the rock and followed the voice. He had never heard anything more beautiful. It was coming from within a forest. He entered the forest and followed the voice until at last he caught sight of the figure of a man wrapped in a white garment with his face turned towards the heavens. His song was one of longing and yearning, and it rose to a glorious cry of love, hope and praise.

The man stopped and turned to the boy, smiling gently. David stepped forward and gazed at the man's eyes.

"You have come," said the man softly. It was the king's Wise Counselor. "Why are you so sad?" he asked the boy.

David began to cry, and told him of all his hopes and expectations and how cruelly they had been disappointed.

"It is true," said the king's Wise Counselor. "The people have been sadly deceived. They have wandered far from the ways of the king, and only when they return will the king himself come back. He promised faithfully that he would return. And so he will. Our task is to prepare the people for his return." And the Wise Counselor explained the whole story of how the people had been led astray from their love of the king and their faith in his promise, and how the Foolish Counselor had usurped the kingdom and dressed up in the clothes of the king.

"But how can the people be brought back?" the boy asked. "Because otherwise the king might never come back."

"I will teach you," said the Wise Counselor. "I can show you something which is greater than any musical instrument you can imagine. Learn to play it and you will have the power to stir men's hearts and bring them to the greatest joy."

"Which instrument is this?" David asked.

"It works with air," the Wise Counselor replied, "with resonating air, just like musical instruments do. You don't play this instrument with your hands. Yet it does have strings of a kind, and by moving them you produce the basic sounds. Then you articulate these sounds with your lips, your teeth, your

tongue, your palate and your throat. I will teach you the secrets of the different sounds. Master this instrument and play it with love. Then you will be able to awaken men's hearts and draw them to the truth. Teach them to play it too and they will draw others to the truth as well. And in the end the whole people will play the most wonderful of songs. They will forget about their troubles and think only of the king. And then he will surely return."

"But where is such an instrument to be found?" asked David.

"It is yours already," replied the king's Wise Counselor smiling. And he pointed with his finger to David's mouth.

Several years passed. David spent the time in the hills with the king's Wise Counselor. He had a small hut in the forest, and there they lived, drinking the waters of mountain streams and eating wild fruits and berries. The Wise Counselor taught David the secrets of the animals and birds; the flowers and the plants and trees; the earth, the sun, the moon and the stars. He taught him about words and language, truth and falsehood, song and joy. And he taught him how to bring light to the hearts of men—with a smile, with encouragement, and with words of truth.

At last David was ready to return to the royal capital. The Wise Counselor wept as he bade him farewell. He handed him a bag of coins and gave him some final words of advice: "Always stand by the truth, because falsehood will never be victorious."

David made his way to the capital.

When he arrived, all the people were hurrying about their daily tasks, rushing from the morning meetings to their jobs, from their jobs to their labor in the orchards, from the orchards to the evening meetings, and then back home to give their tired bodies a few hours of sleep. Their faces were sadder than ever.

David found himself a lodging house, and there he stayed while he went about his task in the city. From morning to evening he would roam the streets, mingling with the crowds as they hurried from place to place. Most people hardly even noticed David as he walked along at a leisurely pace, carrying an old woman's shopping bags for her, perhaps, or helping a mother with her child. Quietly, he would sing melodies — beautiful melodies — and his eyes would move from face to face, smiling gently.

Some of the people who did notice him would quickly glance away — as if they were afraid to be seen smiling. Others stared back curiously as though it were the strangest thing in the world for someone to smile. Some were shocked and disgusted. But one or two would sigh and look back with a tired, sad smile. And David would smile back kindly.

Little by little David became a familiar figure in the city. When people saw him they would even half raise a hand or move their face into the beginnings of a smile, as if to say "Hello." David himself would cheerfully say "Hello" and smile warmly. From time to time he sat on one of the benches by the side of the street. When somebody would sit down beside him, unless he looked as if he would run away like a frightened kitten were David to address him, David might make a comment about the lovely flowers, or the sweet music of the birds.

As the months went by, people looked forward to seeing David. If they happened to find him sitting on one of the benches they might come up and join him. And as they talked about this and that, he might gently introduce the question of *What?*

"*What???*" they would repeat.

"Yes. *What?*" David would answer.

"I don't understand."

"*What* are people doing with their lives?" David would say.

"What do you mean?"

"*What* are they doing? Why are they rushing? What *for*?"

And a little conversation might develop about how everybody seemed to be rushing about from morning till night for the sake of a bit of fruit. But even when they received it, it didn't make them any happier.

"Do you think about your life?" David might ask very gently. And the person would sigh deeply and look down.

After a while the people of the city started asking each other the questions David was asking them.

"Well, the reason we rush around so much is because we've got to work for the fruit," some might answer. "And we have to work for the fruit because we need it to make our lives a bit sweeter. And we need to make our lives sweeter because they're so miserable because we're always in a rush. And we're always in a rush because we've got to work for the fruit. . . ."

"Isn't there a mistake somewhere?" David would ask them softly. "It wasn't always like this, was it? I mean, not when the old king was here"

And when the people heard David mention the old king, they sighed a very deep sigh. Gradually, people began thinking again about the old times when the king had been there.

"But those times are over," they would say sadly.

"Why?" David would ask.

"What do you mean 'why?' He said he's never coming back, didn't he?"

"Who said he's never coming back?"

"Who? What do you mean 'who?' "

"Well, the king himself told us that he would certainly return. So who said he *wouldn't*?"

When David asked this, the people usually became frightened, because they knew it was the Foolish Counselor who

had said the king wasn't coming back. David would continue quietly, "If the master says one thing and the servant another, whom are we to believe — the master or the servant?"

Every night at midnight, when the whole capital was asleep, David would awaken and rise from his bed. Very softly and gently he would begin to sing. It was the song which the king's Wise Counselor had taught him: a song of yearning and longing which rose to a cry of love, hope and praise. And the notes of his song would fly out through his open window and dance about the silent city, darting into the open windows of people's houses and caressing the sleeping citizens of the town. The people would seem to stir for a moment, perhaps, and then turn in their sleep. And a gentle smile would begin to spread upon their faces, healing their souls. And perhaps, as they woke up refreshed in the morning, the little thought would tiptoe into their minds that the old king might possibly be coming back after all.

Now, the king's Foolish Counselor had spies all around city. They came back to the Royal Palace and reported the that a ridiculous rumor was spreading among the people that the old king might change his mind and return. The Foolish Counselor was terrified. He was so exhausted from all his official activities and from the screaming and shouting which accompanied them that he scarcely had the energy to talk any more.

"Who has been spreading these rumors?" he whispered hoarsely. "Catch him! Don't let him escape!"

It was not difficult to find David. He was always out and about the city talking to the people, as it is written: "Wisdom cries aloud in the street: How long, you thoughtless people, will you love thoughtlessness?" (Proverbs 1,20-22). Before long the guards had arrested David, and they brought him before the

Foolish Counselor.

"Who are you and what are you doing here?" the Foolish Counselor croaked. He was so weak now that he had to be carried everywhere in a chair. He sat before David, slumped back in his chair, rubbing his gnarled hands together as if he were trying to keep them warm.

David would not look into the face of the Foolish Counselor. He kept his eyes down and stood patiently in silence.

"What's the matter with you?" said the Foolish Counselor, coughing and spluttering. "Can't you speak? That's always the way. You go around the city telling lies to everyone, but when you're faced with the truth you're silent."

The Foolish Counselor peered forward and looked at David's face, so pure and radiant. And as he did so his hollow eyes began to fill with the beginnings of a tear. He twitched and trembled and tried to clench his fist.

"Well I'm going to teach you a lesson, young man. I'm going to have you put on trial."

And so saying, the Foolish Counselor weakly beckoned to a secretary and ordered him to summon all the Elders to a meeting in the Grand Council Chamber the following morning.

That night something strange happened to the Foolish Counselor. It seemed that his looking and staring at David had given him fresh strength. He lay on his bed propped up on the pillows and gazed at himself in the mirror. His dark, hollow eyes flickered wildly as he beheld the horrible specter that greeted him. There, looking back at him, was the same lurid green face with sunken cheeks that he had always feared so much. It made him feel completely hopeless. A sob welled up in his throat. His heart began to race at the thought of what would happen if the king really *did* come back. He was lost, he thought to himself, whether the king returned or not. He was so unhappy, and he had screamed and screeched and shouted and bawled at so many people that there was nobody left in the world he could call his friend. He had no one at all he could talk to.

Again he thought of David's pure, radiant face—and mysteriously, it inspired him with strength: the strength to weep. When he looked at his haggard face in the mirror, he started sobbing, and he wept and wept until at last he fell asleep.

By morning the Foolish Counselor was already feeling a bit stronger. Although he was carried into the Grand Council Chamber on his usual chair, when the time came for him to address the Elders, instead of remaining seated, he was able to rise to his feet for the first time in months.

"This meeting must be secret," he whispered to the Elders. At once the guards shut the doors, closed all the windows and drew the curtains. Candles were lit. David was led in under guard and made to stand on a platform at the side of Chamber.

The Foolish Counselor raised his gnarled hand and pointed at David as though he were about to say something. But somehow the effort was too much for him. He dropped his hand and slumped down into the chair again. He waited until he had caught his breath, and again he made the effort to stand up, but it seemed that something was crushing his strength, and he fell back into the chair, exhausted. All he could see around him—in the carvings of the walls, on the ornate heads of the pillars, in the shadows under the balcony—all he could see was faces: lurid green faces peering at him and sapping all the life and vitality from his heart.

At last he closed his eyes and shook his head. With a supreme effort he thrust himself out of the chair and stood. He raised his voice in a bitter cry and called out to the Elders: "It's true, my dear Elders, I told you a lie. I said the king would never be coming back, and it was a lie."

And the Foolish Counselor spluttered and sobbed, and he cried and cried and cried.

From deep in the shadows there was a terrible hissing sound, and all the lights went out. The Council Chamber was plunged into darkness. The Foolish Counselor stopped sobbing and began to scream. The king's Enemy was flying around the Council Chamber like a bat and cackling horribly. There was the sound of flapping wings, and a luminous green light flickered on and off and disappeared again into the gloom.

But life was coming back into the Foolish Counselor.

"Look what you've done to me!" he screamed. "You've ruined me! Ruined me!" And he cried out to his guards, "Catch him! The king's Enemy! Catch him!"

It was impossible to see what was happening in the darkness. Suddenly there would be a flash of green light, and the guards would rush over in the direction of the light. But then the sound of cackling would be heard from the other side of the Chamber.

"Form a circle! Form a circle!" a voice was calling. It was David's voice. He cried to the Elders to join him and form a big circle around the Council Chamber.

"Now sing!" David cried. "Dance in a circle and sing to the true king!"

The Elders joined hands and slowly started moving around the Chamber in a circle. They began to sing. The cackling became weaker as they did so, and the king's Enemy flopped on the floor. The guards rushed in to try and catch him, but he was slimy and kept slipping out of their grasp.

"Sing!" cried David. "Sing a song of love and joy to our King!"

Little by little, the Elders raised their voices louder and louder, while the circle began to move faster and faster. As it did so, the king's Enemy became weaker and weaker. His green wrinkled skin began to shrivel and shrink, until it peeled off and dropped to the floor! In place of the king's Enemy a radiant gem was uncovered, spreading its light throughout the Council Chamber.

As the Foolish Counselor sat in his chair weeping, his tears began to wash the furrows and wrinkles from his skin, and little by little the color returned to his cheeks. The Elders were dancing faster and faster and singing with triumphant joy. The Council Chamber was filled with a radiant light. And from the streets came the sounds of cheering and rejoicing.

"Look! Look down the road! There's the carriage! It's the king! He's come back! The king! The king! The king has come back as he promised."

Author's Note

Perhaps some of the people who read this story might be curious to know more about it, so the publisher suggested that I write a few words of explanation.

Parts of the Torah are cast in the form of stories. Our Sages, of blessed memory, also told stories very often in order to teach us things which were difficult to understand. Sometimes they used the components of the story — the characters, the incidents, and the other details — to refer to things very close to us. A king, for example, might stand for God.

The story of "The King Who Came Back" is only a fantasy I spun. I don't know if the story is *correct* in all its details — nor am I wise enough to understand the whole story. If I *could* write the whole story, it would be the story of the Jewish people, whose King — our God — gave us wise rules and wise advisers. God asked us to choose between wisdom — the wisdom of loving and accepting Him and His Divine Laws — and foolishness — the foolishness of doubt which leads to sin. The choices we made have led us to our present situation. The choices we make from now on can lead us to a better future.

A story may describe a certain society or group — or it may portray the mind or soul of a single person. "The King Who Came Back" attempts both of these things. The story seeks to convey a certain picture of the society we live in, and to ask how we reached our present state of affairs. It often seems as if most people are constantly hurrying in search of something and have no time to seek out the truth about themselves or the world. For the truth is that we live in a world where falsehood and foolishness reign. Like the Foolish Counselor, they have seized the position of leadership, and moreover, they have the audacity to *wear the clothes* of truth. All around us we hear *good* words: "This will make you *happy!*"; "It's the *real* thing!"; "Come *alive* with this!" But today, words like "happiness", "reality", "life" and "truth" are often used for things which are no better than depression, fantasy, death and lies.

"The King Who Came Back" is also an attempt to portray the inner mind of a person. Everyone has a good inclination which offers us holy thoughts, good advice and good desires, and an evil inclination which offers us pleasant-seeming strategies which eventually lead us to evil. The more a person listens to the advice of this "Foolish Counselor", the bigger his desires grow and the harder he has to work to achieve them. But in the end he is working so slavishly to fulfill his desires that he cannot enjoy anything! Yet despite the power of falsehood and foolishness, there exists in every person a spark of truth, no matter how deeply it may be buried.

In the story, David had never been touched by the falsehoods of the Foolish Counselor. He had been brought up in simplicity and truth. Thus, he saw immediately that the Foolish Counselor, even while wearing the clothes of the King, could not represent the truth. But even the Foolish Counselor had a point of truth in him. It came to light when he finally wept and admitted how ugly he had become. Until then, he had had no time to look at the truth himself. He was afraid of it, and accordingly, he ran faster and faster so as not to have to think about it. Only when he was able to cry was the vicious cycle broken. Then he could face the truth and be cured.

In the very end, life may get so dark that, just as in the end of the story, hardly anyone will be able to see. Many people may fall prey to terror, thinking that Evil will, God forbid, win the day. But our Sages have taught us that even Evil was created by God as a test for man. When man is able to conquer and vanquish Evil, then out of the very darkness will came a light most radiant.

How far in the future will it be? "Today, if you will listen to His voice" (Psalms 95:7). Today, if we will "search after God with all our heart and soul" (Deut. 4:29).

May the Merciful One make us worthy of the days of Mashiach and the life of the World to Come. Amen.

Avraham ben Yaakov